3 Fun–to–Read–Aloud Stories With a Message

SILLY STORIES

The Standard Publishing Company, Cincinnati, Ohio
A division of Standex International Corporation

07 06 05 04 03 02 01 00   5 4 3 2 1

Library of Congress Catalog Card Number 98-061462
ISBN 0-7847-0820-7

Johnny Thumbs

written by Bob Hartman
illustrated by Richard Max Kolding

There once was a king who loved fine houses. One day the king said, "We will have a contest. The man who builds the finest house will marry the princess."

"What will happen to the losers?" asked the queen.

"We will chop off their heads, of course," said the king.

Most men in the kingdom wanted to keep their heads. So only two men entered the contest.

The first man was Bill Builder. "I will win the contest," he said. "Then people will ask me to build houses for them, too. I will be rich and famous! And I guess I will have to marry the princess."

The second man who entered the contest was Johnny Thumbs. Johnny could not hammer a nail without bashing a finger. Johnny was "all thumbs." That is how he got his name. But Johnny loved the princess with all his heart.

The king gave each man land, bricks, and stones. Bill Builder picked up his tools and started to work. Johnny Thumbs picked up his tools and looked at the princess. He tripped over a wheelbarrow and fell flat on his face. The contest had begun!

One week later, the princess visited Bill Builder and Johnny Thumbs to see how their houses were coming along.

"See my straight walls," said Bill Builder. "See my beautiful window frames. See how well my door opens and closes. No one can build a house like me!"

"Your house is very nice," the princess said. "But if you keep bragging, you will get a big head."

Then the princess went to see Johnny's house. The walls were crooked. The windows were cracked. And Johnny Thumbs was trying to put in the door. When Johnny saw the princess, he bowed. When he bowed, he dropped the door on a stack of wood. The wood flipped into the air and crashed into the wall. The wall fell down on top of Johnny Thumbs. Johnny pulled a brick out of his hat. He shook cement dust out of his ear. "Thank you for coming," he said to the princess. (But he wanted to say, "You are wonderful.") "I will come again," the princess said to Johnny. (But she wanted to say, "You are wonderful, too!")

Another week passed. The princess visited the builders again.

"See my tall roof," said Bill Builder. "See my shiny floors. See my smooth plaster. No one can build a house like me."

"You may be right," said the princess. "But if you keep bragging, you will get a big head."

Then the princess went to see Johnny's house. Johnny Thumbs was working on the roof. When he saw the princess, he lost his balance and fell off. He knocked down his ladder. He knocked down bundles of sticks and straw. Johnny pulled a ladder rung out of his hat. He shook bits of straw out of his ear. Then Johnny heard the princess calling for help. So he dug her out from under a pile of sticks and straw. "I am so sorry," he said. (But he wanted to say, "You look beautiful.")

"That is all right," the princess answered. (But she wanted to say, "You are very kind and brave. Even if you are very clumsy.")

Another week went by. The contest was over. The king and queen and the princess came to look at both houses. One large soldier with a very sharp axe came, too.

"Come in!" called Bill Builder. "Come into the finest house in all the land! See my beautiful furniture," Bill Builder said. "See my fancy carpets and lovely curtains."

"Ooh!" said the king.

"Aah!" said the queen.

"Pretty!" said the soldier with the very sharp axe.

Bill Builder smiled. No one could build a house like him.

Just then there was a puffing sound. "Ooh!" said the princess. "Aah!" said the soldier.

What are they oohing and aahing about? Bill Builder wondered. I have not finished telling them about my house. Suddenly Bill Builder felt his head bump against the ceiling.

"I warned you not to get a big head," said the princess.

Bill Builder's head crashed through the ceiling into the second floor. "Run!" shouted the king.

"Wait!" called Bill Builder. "See my fine staircase! See my strong chimney!"

The more Bill Builder bragged, the bigger his head grew. Soon his hair touched the rafters. Soon his ears pressed against the walls.

"No one can build a house like me!" he yelled. Then the house fell down around him with a crash.

"Bill Builder's house was a fine house," said the king. "But the princess cannot live there now." So the king and queen and the princess and the soldier went to see the house that Johnny built.

When they arrived, Johnny Thumbs bowed and said, "Welcome." But the king took one look at Johnny's house and said, "This house is not fit for the princess, either." The soldier with the axe stepped forward.

"Please, Father," said the princess. "Give Johnny Thumbs a chance. Just go inside." So the king and queen went inside.

"You are beautiful," Johnny whispered to the princess.

"You are brave and kind," the princess whispered back.

"There is something special about this house," said the king. "What is it?"

"I love you," Johnny whispered to the princess.

"I love you, too," the princess whispered back.

"That is it!" shouted the king. "This house was built with love! Love makes this house the finest house in all my kingdom!" Johnny Thumbs had won the contest.

The next day, Johnny and the princess were married. They moved into Johnny's house and lived happily ever after.

As for Bill Builder, the king could not find an axe large enough to chop off his head. So Bill Builder wandered around the kingdom.

"No one can build a house like me!" he shouted. And he is *still* looking for a hat big enough to cover his big head.

JESSICA JACOBS DID WHAT?

written by Nancy Ellen Hird
illustrated by Andy Stiles

Jessica Jacobs turned her head sharply to the clock on the classroom wall.

"The bus for the field trip leaves in five minutes," she said.

"Your mom will get here," said Sam.

Jessica tried to smile. Sam and all the other third graders got up to leave for the bus. Jessica's mother poked her head into the room.

"Whew!" said Jessica. She jumped up.

"Here is your permission slip," said Mrs. Jacobs.

"Now I can go," said Jessica. "Thanks, Mom, for bringing it." She zipped up her coat.

"And," said Mrs. Jacobs, "here is your lunch."

"I forgot that, too?" asked Jessica.

Mrs. Jacobs rolled her eyes. "Yes, and this is the third time this week," she said. "I think you would forget your head if it were not on your neck."

Jessica giggled and touched her head. "It's still there," she said.

"So far," said her mother with a smile.

Jessica kissed her mother and ran to the waiting bus. She got in line behind her friend Sam. "I got it!" Jessica said. She waved her permission slip.

"Great," said Sam. "Was your mom mad?"

"No," said Jessica, "but I hope I don't forget anything else."

"Did you ask her if you can come to my party tomorrow night?"

"Oops," said Jessica. She pulled the invitation from the pocket of her jeans. "I forgot."

Ring! R-r-ring!

The next morning, Jessica reached out and shut off her alarm clock. Slowly she walked to the bathroom.

She turned on the water. She looked in the mirror. She saw her blue nightgown. She saw her neck. But on top of her neck there was . . .

The mirror is just fogged up, thought Jessica. She rubbed the mirror with her hand. Jessica looked in the mirror again. Oh, no! she thought. Where is my head? And if I don't have a head, how can I still see and hear?

There was a knock on the door. "Jessica," called Mrs. Jacobs, "don't let the water run." Jessica turned off the water. She did not want her mother to come in. She did not want her mother to see her like this. Jessica wondered what to do. Well, she thought, I guess I don't have to wash my face!

Jessica opened the bathroom door. She peeked out. She heard bowls clinking. Good, she thought. Mom is in the kitchen. Jessica ran to her room and closed the door behind her.

My head must be here someplace, thought Jessica. She looked under the bed. She found a sock, a math paper, a missing library book, her sunglasses, but no head.

She looked in her closet. But still she did not find her head. "What am I going to do?" she wondered. "I have to go to school."

Jessica put on her jeans and a sweater. She wrapped a long scarf up and over her neck. She put a big floppy hat on top. She stuck her sunglasses into the scarf. Maybe, she thought, no one will notice.

Jessica walked into class.

Willy Cook laughed and pointed at her hat. "Hey, Jessica," he said. "Are you going to the beach today?"

"Please take your seats," said Mr. Ramos. "The heater is not working well, so keep on your coats. And your hats."

Whew! thought Jessica.

"Here is my half of our report," said Sam. "See, I wrote it neatly. Now it will be easy for you to read to the class."

Oh, no! thought Jessica. We have to give our report after lunch. I forgot!

Jessica got out a pencil and a piece of paper. "Can't talk," she wrote. Sam's eyes got big.

"But you have to," he said. "Why can't you?"

Jessica just pointed to the words on the paper.

"I can't read in front of the class," said Sam. "I will get sick. But if we don't give our report—"

Jessica slid down in her seat. What more could go wrong? she worried.

After recess, Mr. Ramos said, "The room is warm now. You may all take off your coats and hats and hang them up.

Jessica hung up her coat. What should I do about my hat? she wondered.

Jessica went back to her seat.

"Jessica," said Mr. Ramos, "you didn't take off your hat." Jessica did not move. Mr. Ramos came closer. What is he going to do? thought Jessica.

"Is there a reason," Mr. Ramos asked, "why you can't take off your hat?" Everyone looked at Jessica.

Jessica did not move. Mr. Ramos frowned. "Go to the principal's office," he said. "I will come at lunchtime. We will talk then."

Jessica sat in the principal's office. What am I going to do? she wondered. How can I face Mr. Ramos without a face?

Then the door opened. Jessica stared. Oh, no! she thought. It's not Mr. Ramos. It's Mom! Jessica leaned back in her chair. She tried to make herself very small.

"Hi, Miss Bell," said Mrs. Jacobs to the school secretary. "I have something for Jessica. May I go to her classroom?"

"Yes," said Miss Bell, "but Jessica is here."

Mrs. Jacobs turned. Her mouth fell open. Then she smiled. "I think you need this," she said. Mrs. Jacobs gave Jessica a brown paper bag.

Jessica took the big bag. It was too heavy to be her lunch. She looked inside the bag. There was her head! Jessica pulled it out of the bag right away. Then she remembered Miss Bell. What will Miss Bell say? Jessica worried. Will she faint?

Jessica looked up. Miss Bell was smiling. "This happens to at least one third grader every year," Miss Bell said.

Jessica put on her head. "Thanks, Mom," she said.

"I wish you had told me about this," said Mrs. Jacobs.

"I was afraid you would be mad," said Jessica.

Mrs. Jacobs smiled. "Maybe," she said. "But I love you. And I will always help you if I can. So please ask next time." Jessica nodded a big nod.

Then Jessica remembered the invitation to Sam's party. She pulled it out of her pocket and gave it to her mother. "Jessica," said Mrs. Jacobs, "this party is tonight!"

"I know," said Jessica. "I'm sorry. I forgot to tell you."

Mrs. Jacobs shook her head. Then she smiled and put her hand on Jessica's shoulder. "OK," she said. "What gift would Sam like?"

Aunt Mabel's Table

written by Bob Hartman
illustrated by Richard Max Kolding

There were five cans on Aunt Mabel's table. One for Aunt Mabel. One for my cousin Sue. One for Uncle Joe. One for my cousin Tom. And one for me, Alexander. Yes, there were five cans on Aunt Mabel's table. And not one of them had a label.

"I got them on sale at the supermarket!" said Aunt Mabel.

"This is a game we play," whispered Sue.

"You have to eat whatever is in your can," sighed Uncle Joe.

"I got dog food last time," laughed Tom.

I want to go home, I thought. And then I remembered what my mother had said: "Your aunt Mabel is a little funny. Just try to be polite."

There were five cans on Aunt Mabel's table. "I am the oldest," said Aunt Mabel. "So I get to go first." Aunt Mabel picked up the biggest can. She looked at its top and at its bottom. She looked all around its sides. Then she held it to her ear and shook it. Everybody listened.

"Sounds like sweet yellow peaches," guessed Aunt Mabel.

"Sounds like round red tomatoes," guessed Sue.

"Sounds like tiny white potatoes," guessed Uncle Joe. "The kind that make me sneeze."

"Sounds like dog food," guessed Tom.

"I don't know," I said. "It just sounds all splashy and splooshy to me."

Aunt Mabel banged the can on the kitchen counter. She pulled a can opener out of a drawer. She cranked off the lid in a flash. Then she held the can in the air and smiled. "Peaches!" she said, "I love peaches!"

There were four cans on Aunt Mabel's table. My cousin Sue took the smallest. She looked at its top and at its bottom. She looked all around its sides. Then she held it to her ear and shook it. Everybody listened.

"Sounds like soft flaky tuna," guessed Aunt Mabel.

"Or yummy pink salmon," guessed Sue.

"Sounds like that lumpy meat spread," guessed Uncle Joe. "The kind that makes me burp."

"Sounds like dog food," teased Tom.

"I don't know," I said. "It just sounds all soft and squishy to me."

Sue placed the can on the counter and opened it carefully. She turned around with the can in her hands and an awful look on her face. "Mushrooms," she moaned. "I hate mushrooms!"

There were three cans on Aunt Mabel's table. They were all about the same size now. Uncle Joe sighed and took the one in the middle. He looked at its top and at its bottom. He looked all around its sides. Then he held it to his ear and shook it. Everybody listened.

"Sounds like long stringy beans," guessed Aunt Mabel.

"Sounds like creamed corn," guessed Sue.

"Sounds like those kidney beans you always buy," guessed Uncle Joe. "The kind that make me itch."

"Sounds like dog food," guessed Tom.

"Sounds like . . . peas?" I said with a shrug. I was trying to be polite.

Uncle Joe put the can on the counter. But he had trouble opening it. "Hurry!" shouted Aunt Mabel. "This is so exciting!"

At last, Uncle Joe got the lid off. He turned around and sighed. "Kidney beans," he said. "I itch already."

There were two cans on Aunt Mabel's table. Tom picked up the one without a dent. He looked at its top and at its bottom. He looked all around its sides. Then he held it to his ear and shook it. Everybody listened.

"Sounds like pork and beans," guessed Aunt Mabel.

"Sounds like cranberry sauce," guessed Sue.

"Sounds like thick soup, " guessed Uncle Joe. "The kind you add water to."

"It had better not be dog food," said Tom.

"Sounds like spaghetti!" I guessed. I was catching on.

Tom opened the can as quickly as he could, just to get it over with. But before he could turn around, I stuck my head over his shoulder and peeked.

"I was right!" I shouted. "It is spaghetti!"

"I hate spaghetti," said Tom.

There was one can left on Aunt Mabel's table. I swallowed hard and picked it up. If I was going to be polite, I would have to eat whatever was in it. I looked at its top and at its bottom. I looked all around its dented sides. Then I held it to my ear and shook it. It made no sound at all.

For the first time, Aunt Mabel looked serious. "It could very well be dog food," she guessed.

"Or cat food," guessed Sue.

"Probably beef and liver flavor," guessed Uncle Joe. "The kind that smells so bad."

"Bow-wow," barked Tom.

I said nothing.

I put the can on the counter. I stuck the sharp bit of the can opener into the top and started to turn the handle. I turned the handle ten times. Then I carefully pulled up the lid of the can. What I saw inside was brown and thick and gooey. It was a whole can of chocolate pudding!

There were five of us at Aunt Mabel's table. Aunt Mabel stuck a big spoon into her bowl of peaches. "Thank you for coming to dinner," she said to me.

My cousin Sue looked at her plate of mushrooms and said nothing.

My Uncle Joe stared at his dish of kidney beans and started scratching.

My older cousin Tom asked to leave the room.

But I remembered what my mother had told me. "Thank you for having me," I said. Then I stuck a big spoon into my chocolate pudding and ate it all up. I was very polite!